This book belongs to

"The NSPCC is pleased to work with Egmont World on the development of this series of story books. We believe that they will help parents better understand their children's needs and help children cope with a variety of social issues."
Jim Harding, Chief Executive, NSPCC.

The NSPCC Happy Kids logo and Happy Kids characters:
TM & © NSPCC 2000. Licensed by CPL
NSPCC Registered Charity Number: 216401

Published in Great Britain by Egmont World Ltd.,
Deanway Technology Centre, Wilmslow Road, Handforth,
Cheshire, SK9 3FB. Printed in Italy
ISBN PBK 0 7498 4640 2
ISBN HBK 0 7498 4735 2
A catalogue record for this book is available from the British Library.

One day the Happy Kids were at the
After School Club.
There were lots of things to do.
Jordan was playing a computer game.

Emily and some other children had discovered a big box of very old toys right at the back of the cupboard.

Spike was happy playing a game with one of his friends.

Then Spike's friend's mum said, "Time to go!"
and Spike was left all by himself.

"Oh no!" thought Spike. "My dad won't be here for ages. What am I going to do now? I want to go home."

"Do you want to play this game with me?" he asked Jordan.

VROOOM

But Jordan was busy. "Can't stop now!" he said. "I'm nearly on the next level!"

Spike slumped in front of the television. One of his favourite programmes was on, but it didn't seem all that good now that he was watching it all by himself.

He could hear Jordan shouting.
He could hear the computer going:

VVRROOOOMMM!

BRRRM!

BRRM

He could hear Emily's loud laughs and the
other children chatting and giggling.

He wandered over to see what they were doing.

"Do you want to play footy?" he asked.

Emily laughed at him. "Don't be silly," she said.

"We can't play ball in here!"

Jody and Maya giggled.

"You can play with us, if you like," Maya said. And she showed him the very big box of scruffy teds, battered bunnies, one-eyed pandas and wonky kittens.

Now it was Spike's turn to laugh.
"I think that's a silly game!" he said.
And he stomped off.

Oh!
The poor thing.

Spike wandered about gloomily.
Everybody was busy playing
except him. He could hear Jordan
getting more and more excited
with his game. He could hear
Emily's loud laugh.

Are you laughing at me?

He thought he heard Maya saying, "Oh! The poor thing," and giggling.

Spike couldn't stand it anymore.
"Are you laughing at me?" he said.

He grabbed one of their scruffy toys.
It was a very old rabbit with one
loose eye and a wonky ear.
Spike grabbed it and held it high
over his head.
"Look at this," he said.
"It's rubbish! It's falling apart!"

And then …

The rabbit did fall apart!
Its floppy body fell to the ground.
Its loose eye rolled away.
Spike was left holding one tattered toy
rabbit's ear high up over his head.
"Oh!" he said.

Look what you've done!

screamed the children.

Jordan came up. He'd finished his game. "You should have seen my score!" he said.

Then he saw what had happened. "Oh," he said too.

Spike was still standing there holding the ear.
Maya was sniffing and looking unhappy.

Emily was glaring
at Spike.

Jody looked
cross too.

"I didn't mean to break it!
I'm sorry," Spike said.

"Maybe we can fix it,"
suggested Jordan.

Then "I've got an idea!"
Spike said,
and he rushed off.

Soon he was back with the box of bits
the children used for making things.
It was full of papers and bits of rag
and cloth and sticky tape.

"Look!" he said.

"Go away. We don't want to make things," Emily grumbled.

"Just listen," said Spike. And he told them all about his idea.

He used sticky tape on the rabbit's ear.
Then he wound a cloth round the rabbit's head.
"There!" said Spike. "It's been to the
animal hospital."
"I want to be a vet too," said Emily.
She started bandaging up the toys
and making beds for them.
"I'll find some more sick pets," said Jordan.
He started to look for toys they could bandage.
"I'll be the reception lady," said Jody.
"Everyone wait here please.
Take a seat, Jordan!"

For the rest of the club time they all
played together.
Nobody felt left out. Nobody felt cross.
And all the scruffy teds, battered bunnies
and wonky kittens looked
much much better!

ALL TOGETHER NOW — A STORY ABOUT BEING FRIENDS

Advice to Parents and Carers

As well as providing tales which will entertain children, this series of stories about the Happy Kids illustrates how we should treat and care for each other. When your child has read the story or you have read it with him or her, you may wish to discuss the issues raised. Find a quiet place and be prepared to spend a little time together. Let your child ask any questions he or she likes arising from the story.

This story about the Happy Kids raises questions about friendships and how children treat each other. Parents may be concerned about how their children form friendships but remember that with 5 to 11 year olds friendships can often be short-lived and children move in and out of them quite quickly. While parents can help in the process of their children making friends, also remember that children have different needs and that it is really children who will make their own choices. Parents can, however, provide situations in which friendships can develop – for example, through taking children to places where other children meet and play together and through inviting children home.

- Welcome your child's friends into your home and show interest in them. This will help them get on together.
- Encourage your children to have friends of each sex. This will help them when they are older.
- It's best if friends are of a similar age. If you child's friends are either significantly older or younger, check how they are getting on.
- Don't show your children up in front of their friends!
- We all need to work at friendships – they don't just happen. Parents can talk to their children about this in terms of their own friendships.

If you want to talk through parenting issues of this sort you can phone Parentline on:
0808 800 2222 (Textphone: 0800 783 6783).

If you are a parent, carer, or relative and need advice or help on these or related issues or are concerned about a child and don't know what to do for the best you can always call the NSPCC Child Protection Helpline. This is a free service, open 24 hours a day, 365 days a year. A qualified social work counsellor will listen to you and take your concerns seriously.

NSPCC
CHILD PROTECTION
HELPLINE
0800 800 500
TEXTPHONE 0800 056 0566

Special Offers for Happy Kids readers

Thank you for purchasing this NSPCC Happy Kids story book, which will automatically generate a contribution to the NSPCC cause, to help more children become happier children.

We've also got some special gift offers for Happy Kids readers.
This six-piece school set is available for only £2.50 and includes a pencil case, two pencils and a sharpener, an eraser and 15cm ruler – all items featuring the Happy Kids characters.

Simply send a cheque for only £2.50 (inc. post and package) to
NSPCC Happy Kids,
Marketing Department (6pcs),
Egmont World Ltd, PO Box 7,
Manchester MI9 2HD.
Please include your name and address including postcode and allow 28 days for delivery. We will then give 10p from the sale of each School Set to the NSPCC.

Thank you

We are the Happy Kids!